Praise for  W9-CCM-593

PHILIP PULLMAN'S
The Firework-Maker's Daughter

★"Reminiscent, in spirit, of Lloyd Alexander's tales, with their strong, clever heroines, this story is abundantly good-natured and rich with humorous scenes and philosophical underpinnings. Pullman portrays his main characters deftly, sets them in a colorful, convincing world, and brings the story to a memorable climax."

—*Booklist*, starred review

"This comical adventure crackles with Pullman's usual flair. ...Pullman marries elements of fairy tale with slapstick humor. Gallagher's softly focused graphite drawings lend magical mystery."

—*Publishers Weekly*

"Characteristically, Pullman builds anticipation to a breathtaking conclusion, while Gallagher's distinctive black-and-white illustrations lead readers on a fantastical journey fraught with danger and a dream realized."

—*Kirkus Reviews*

"Stately but expressive graphite drawings open each chapter and add to the expanded folktale feel of this story. This one will be remembered for its broad humor and gentle moral. Readers will see, hear, smell, and be dazzled by the fireworks that burst forth."

—*School Library Journal*

"Pullman's talent for imagery sparks to life and the fast pace guarantees a breathless adventure."
—*Bulletin of the Center for Children's Books*

"This story will find an eager audience who will appreciate the brave heroine, her steadfast friend, and their adventures. The writing is spirited, the fireworks are lively, and the characters are a treat."

—*VOYA*

"Pullman, a master storyteller, has created an exciting coming-of-age story of courage, love, and friendship.... Pullman's clever and determined female protagonist communicates the message that girls should be judged by their talents, not their sex. Pullman's many fans will enjoy this charming tale."

—*The Book Report*

Booklist Editors' Choice

Other Signature Titles

Clockwork
Philip Pullman

Ghost Cats
Susan Shreve

Riding Freedom
Pam Muñoz Ryan

Just Juice
Karen Hesse

Faith and the Rocket Cat
Patrick Jennings

Faith and the Electric Dog
Patrick Jennings

The firework-Maker's Daughter

Illustrations by
S. Saelig Gallagher

The firework-Maker's Daughter

by Philip Pullman

**SCHOLASTIC
SIGNATURE**

an imprint of
Scholastic Inc.

New York Toronto London Auckland Sydney
Mexico City New Delhi Hong Kong

No part of this publication may be reproduced
in whole or in part, or stored in a retrieval system,
or transmitted in any form or by any means, electronic,
mechanical, photocopying, recording, or otherwise, without written
permission of the publisher. For information regarding permission,
write to Scholastic Inc., Attention: Permissions Department,
555 Broadway, New York, NY 10012.

ISBN 0-590-12943-0
((LC #)) 98-41048

Text copyright © 1995 by Philip Pullman.
Illustrations copyright © 1995 by S. Saelig Gallagher.
All rights reserved. Published by Scholastic Inc.
SCHOLASTIC, the LANTERN LOGO, and associated logos are
trademarks and/or registered trademarks of Scholastic Inc.

12 11 10 9 8 7 6 5 4 3 2   1 2 3 4 5/0

Printed in the U.S.A.   40

First Scholastic paperback printing, November 2000

Original hardcover edition designed by
Elizabeth Parisi, published by
Arthur A. Levine Books,
an imprint of Scholastic Press,
October 1999.

Contents

The firework-Maker's Daughter

The Firework-Maker's Daughter

A thousand miles ago, in a country east of the
jungle and south of the mountains, there lived a firework-
maker called Lalchand and his daughter, Lila.

Lalchand's wife had died when Lila was young. The
child was a cross little thing, always crying and refusing
her food, but Lalchand built a cradle for her in the corner
of the workshop, where she could see the sparks play and
listen to the fizz and crackle of the gunpowder. Once she
was out of her cradle, she toddled around the workshop
laughing as the fire flared and the sparks danced. Many a
time she burned her little fingers, but Lalchand splashed
water on them and kissed her better, and soon she was
playing again.

When she was old enough to learn, her father began
to teach her the art of making fireworks. She began with

There were a lot of thoughts flying around in my head, none of which I could actually get a handle on. We both sat there in silence until the buzzer from the oven went off, telling me that my pizza was done. I wanted to say something intelligent to show my father I understood, but all I could think of to say was "Would you like a slice of pizza?" Even though it wasn't very profound, I think my father understood.

little Crackle Dragons, six on a string. Then she learned how to make Leaping Monkeys, Golden Sneezes, and Java Lights. Soon she was making all the simple fireworks, and thinking about more complicated ones.

One day she said, "Father, if I put some flowers of salt in a Java Light instead of cloud powder, what would happen?"

"Try it and see," he said.

So she did. Instead of burning with a steady green glimmer, it sprayed out wicked little sparks, each of which turned a somersault before going out.

"Not bad, Lila," said Lalchand. "What are you going to call it?"

"Mmm . . . Tumbling Demons," she said.

"Excellent! Make a dozen and we'll put them into the New Year Festival display."

The Tumbling Demons were a great success, and so were the Shimmering Coins that Lila invented next. As time went on she learned more and more of her father's art, until one day she said, "Am I a proper fireworkmaker now?"

"No, no," he said. "By no means. Ha! You don't know

the start of it. What are the ingredients of flyaway powder?"

"I don't know."

"And where do you find thunder grains?"

"I've never heard of thunder grains."

"How much scorpion oil do you put in a Krakatoa Fountain?"

"A teaspoonful?"

"*What?* You'd blow up the whole city. You've got a lot to learn yet. Do you really want to be a firework-maker, Lila?"

"Of course I do! It's the only thing I want!"

"I was afraid so," he said. "It's my own fault. What was I thinking of? I should have sent you to my sister Jembavati to bring up as a dancer. This is no place for a girl, and just look at you, now I come to think of it, your hair's a mess, your fingers are burned and stained with chemicals, your eyebrows are scorched. . . . How am I going to find a husband for you when you look like that?"

Lila was horrified.

"A *husband*?"

"Well, of course! You don't imagine you can stay here forever, do you?"

They looked at each other as if they were strangers. Each of them had had quite the wrong idea about things, and they were both alarmed to find it out.

So Lila said no more about being a firework-maker, and Lalchand said no more about husbands. But they both thought about them, all the same.

Now the king of that country owned a white elephant. It was the custom that whenever the king wanted to punish one of his courtiers, he would send him the white elephant as a present, and the expense of looking after the animal would ruin the poor man — because the white elephant had to sleep between silk sheets (enormous ones), and eat mango-flavored Turkish Delight (tons of it), and have his tusks covered in gold leaf every morning. When the courtier had no money left at all, the white elephant would be returned to the king, ready for his next victim.

Wherever the white elephant went, his personal servant had to go too. The servant's name was Chulak, and he was the same age as Lila. In fact, they were friends. Every afternoon, Chulak would take the white elephant

out for his exercise, because the elephant would go with no one else, and there was a reason for this: Chulak was the only person, besides Lila, who knew that the elephant could talk.

One day Lila went to visit Chulak and the white elephant. She arrived at the elephant house in time to hear the elephant master losing his temper.

"You horrible little boy!" he roared. "You've done it again, haven't you?"

"Done what?" said Chulak innocently.

"Look!" said the elephant master, pointing with a quivering finger at the white elephant's snowy flanks.

Written all over his side in charcoal and paint were dozens of slogans:

EAT AT THE GOLDEN LANTERN

BANGKOK WANDERERS FOR THE CUP

STAR OF INDIA TANDOORI HOUSE

And right at the very top of the white elephant's back, in letters a foot high:

CHANG LOVES LOTUS BLOSSOM <u>TRUE</u> XXX

"Every day this elephant comes home with graffiti all over him!" shouted the elephant master. "Why don't you stop people from doing it?"

"I can't understand how it happens, master," said Chulak. "Mind you, the traffic's awful. I've got to watch these rickshaw drivers like a hawk. I can't look out for graffiti artists as well — they just slap it up and run."

"But CHANG LOVES LOTUS BLOSSOM <u>TRUE</u> must have taken a good ten minutes on a stepladder!"

"Yes, it's a mystery to me, master. Shall I clean it off?"

"All of it! There's a job coming up in a day or two, and I want this animal *clean*."

And the elephant master stormed off, leaving Chulak and Lila with the elephant.

"Hello, Hamlet," said Lila.

"Hello, Lila," sighed the elephant. "Look what this obnoxious brat has reduced me to! A walking billboard!"

"Stop fussing," said Chulak. "Look, we've got eighteen rupees already — and ten annas from the Tandoori House — and Chang gave me a whole rupee for letting him write that on the top — we're nearly there, Hamlet!"

"The *shame*!" said Hamlet, shaking his great head.

"You mean you charge people money to write on him?" said Lila.

"Course!" said Chulak. "It's dead lucky to write your name on a white elephant. When we've got enough, we're going to run away. Trouble is, he's in love with a lady elephant at the zoo. You ought to see him blush when we go past — like a ton of strawberry ice cream!"

"She's called Frangipani," said Hamlet mournfully. "But she won't even look at me. And now there's another

job coming up — another poor man to bankrupt — oh, I hate Turkish Delight! I detest silk sheets! And I loathe gold leaf on my tusks! I wish I was a normal dull gray elephant!"

"No, you don't," said Chulak. "We've got plans, Hamlet, remember. I'm teaching him to sing, Lila. We'll change his name to Luciano Elephanti, and the world'll be our oyster."

"But why are you looking so sad, Lila?" said Hamlet, as Chulak began to scrub him down.

"My father won't tell me the final secret of firework-making," said Lila. "I've learned all there is to know about flyaway powder and thunder grains, and scorpion oil and spark repellent, and glimmer juice and salts-of-shadow, but there's something else I need to know, and he won't tell me."

"Tricky," said Chulak. "Shall I ask him for you?"

"If he won't tell me, he certainly won't tell you," said Lila.

"He won't know he's doing it," said Chulak. "You leave it to me."

So that evening, after he'd settled Hamlet down for the night, Chulak called at the firework-maker's work-

shop. It lay down a little winding alley full of crackling smells and pungent noises, between the fried-prawn stall and the batik painter's. He found Lalchand in the courtyard under the warm stars, mixing up some red glow paste.

"Hello, Chulak," said Lalchand. "I hear the white elephant's going to be presented to Lord Parakit tomorrow. How long d'you think his money'll last?"

"A week, I reckon," said Chulak. "Though you never know — we might run away before then. I've nearly got enough to get us to India. I thought I might take up firework-making when we got there. Nice trade."

"Nice trade my foot!" said Lalchand. "Firework-making is a sacred art! You need talent and dedication and the favor of the gods before you can become a firework-maker. The only thing *you're* dedicated to is idleness, you scamp."

"How did you become a firework-maker, then?"

"I was apprenticed to my father. And then I had to be tested to see whether I had the Three Gifts."

"Oh, the Three Gifts, eh," said Chulak, who had no idea what the Three Gifts were. *Probably Lila did,* he thought. "And did you have them?"

"Of course I did!"

"And that's it? Sounds easy. I bet I could pass that test. I've got a lot more than three gifts."

"Pah!" said Lalchand. "That's not all. Then came the most difficult and dangerous part of the whole apprenticeship. Every firework-maker —" and he lowered his voice and looked around to make sure no one was listening — "every firework-maker has to travel to the Grotto of Razvani the Fire-Fiend, in the heart of Mount Merapi, and exchange the Three Gifts for some of the royal sulphur. That's the ingredient that makes the finest fireworks. Without that, no one can ever be a true firework-maker."

"Ah," said Chulak. "Royal sulphur. Mount Merapi. That's the volcano, isn't it?"

"Yes, you pestilential boy, and already I've told you far more than I should. This is a secret, you understand?"

"Of course," said Chulak, looking solemn. "I can keep a secret."

And Lalchand had the uneasy feeling that he'd been tricked, though he couldn't imagine why.

Escape

Next morning, while Lalchand was at the paper merchant's buying some cardboard tubes, Lila went to the elephant house to see Chulak. When she heard what Lalchand had told him, she was furious.

"Mount Merapi — Razvani — the royal sulphur — and he wasn't going to tell me! Oh, I'll never forgive him!"

"That's a bit drastic," said Chulak, who was busy getting the elephant ready for a new job. "He's only thinking of you. It's dangerous, after all. You wouldn't catch me going up there."

"Huh!" she said. "It's all right to let me make Golden Sneezes and Java Lights, I suppose, little baby things. But not to let me become a real firework-maker. He wants me to stay a child for ever. Well, I'm not going to, Chulak, I've had enough. I'm going to Mount Merapi,

and I'm going to bring back the royal sulphur, and I'll set up as a firework-maker on my own and put my father out of business. You see if I don't."

"No! Wait! You ought to talk to him —"

But Lila wouldn't listen. She ran straight home, packed a little food to eat and blanket and a few bronze coins, and left a note on the workshop bench:

> Dear Father,
> I have completed my apprenticeship. Thank you for all you have taught me. I am going to seek the royal sulphur from Razvani the Fire-Fiend, and I shall probably not see you again.
>
> Your ex-daughter, Lila

Then she thought she should take something to show Razvani her skill, and packed a few self-igniting Crackle Dragons. One of the last things she had invented was a new way of setting them off: You just had to pull a string instead of setting light to them, because the string was soaked with a solution of fire-crystals. She put three of them in her bag, took one last look around the workshop, and slipped away.

When Lalchand came back and found her note, he read it with horror.

"Oh, Lila, Lila! You don't know what you're doing!" he cried, and ran out into the alley.

"Have you seen Lila?" he asked the fried-prawn seller.

"She went off in that direction. About half an hour ago."

"She had a bundle on her back," added the batik painter. "Looked as if she was going on a journey."

Lalchand hurried after her at once. But he was an old man with a weak heart, and he couldn't run fast, and the streets were crowded: rickshaw drivers jostled with bullock carts, a caravan of silk traders was pushing its way through the market, and in the Grand Boulevard, a procession was going past. The crowd was so thick that Lalchand couldn't move any further.

The reason for all the excitement was that the white elephant was being led to his new owner. Chulak was at the head of the procession, leading Hamlet with a golden chain, and behind them came musicians playing bamboo flutes and banging teak drums, and dancers swaying and snapping their fingernails, and a troop of servants with

tape measures, ready to measure Hamlet's new home for
the silk curtains and velvet carpets the owner would have
to buy. Flags flapped and banners waved in the sunlight,
and the white elephant shone like a snowy mountain.

Lalchand forced his way through the crowd to
Chulak's side.

"Did you tell Lila about Razvani and the royal sulphur?" he panted.

"Course," said Chulak. "You should have told her
yourself. Why?"

"Because she's gone, you wretch! She's gone off by
herself to Mount Merapi — and she doesn't know the
rest of the secret!"

"Is there more, then?"

"Of course there is!" said Lalchand, struggling to
keep up. "No one can go into the fire-fiend's grotto without protection. She needs a flask of magic water from the
Goddess of the Emerald Lake — otherwise she'll perish
in the flames! Oh, Chulak, what have you done?"

Chulak gulped. They were nearly at the house of the
white elephant's new owner, and they had to slow down
to allow all the dancers and musicians and flag bearers to

get through the gate first and form two lines for the white elephant to walk between.

Then Hamlet whispered, just loud enough for Chulak to hear, "I'll find her! Help me get away tonight, Chulak, and we'll go and take Lila the magic water."

"Good idea," whispered Chulak, beaming. "Just what I was going to suggest." He turned to Lalchand and said, "Listen, I got a proposition. Me and Hamlet'll find her! We'll get out tonight. Emerald Lake — Goddess — magic water — Mount Merapi! Nothing to it."

Then Chulak turned to the servants.

"Get out of the way," he called, "we got to get him around the corner — tsk, tsk, what a narrow gate! That'll have to come down. And what's this? *Gravel?* You want the white elephant to walk on *gravel?* Fetch a carpet at once! A red one! Go on! Hurry!"

He clapped his hands, and the servants bowed and scampered away. In the background the new owner was tearing his hair. Chulak whispered to Lalchand once more:

"Don't worry! We'll get away tonight. All we need is a tarpaulin."

"A tarpaulin? Whatever for?"

"No time to explain now. Just bring one to the gate tonight."

And Lalchand had to make do with that. He went back to the workshop feeling heavyhearted.

All this while, Lila had been making her way through the jungle toward the sacred volcano. Mount Merapi lay far to the north, and she had never seen it until, late that afternoon, she came to a bend in the jungle path, and found herself beside the river.

The size of the great mountain made her gasp. It was far away on the very edge of the world, but even so it reached halfway up the sky, with the bare sides rising in a perfect cone to the glowing crater at the top. From time to time the fire-spirits who lived there rumbled angrily underground and threw boiling rocks high into the air. A plume of eternal smoke drifted from the summit to join the clouds.

How can I ever get there? she wondered, and felt her heart quail. But she had chosen to make the journey, and she could hardly turn back when she'd only just begun. She shifted her bundle from one shoulder to the other and walked on.

The jungle was a noisy place. Monkeys gibbered in the trees, and parrots screeched, and crocodiles snapped their jaws in the river. Every so often Lila had to step carefully over a snake sleeping in the sun, and once she heard the roar of a mighty tiger. There was no one to be seen except some fishermen laboriously rowing their boat across from the other side of the river.

She stopped and watched as they brought their boat in toward the bank where she was standing. They weren't making very good progress. There were six or

seven of them, and all their oars were getting in one another's way. As she watched, one of the fishermen missed the water completely with his oar, which swung around and clumped another fisherman on the head. That fisherman turned around and punched the first one, who fell off his seat with a squeal and dropped the oar in the water. One of the others tried to grab it, but instead he fell out of the boat, which rocked so violently that the others all cried out in alarm and grabbed the sides.

The man who'd fallen out was splashing and spluttering as he tried to climb back into the boat, and all the crocodiles basking in the shallows looked up, interested. Lila caught her breath in alarm, but the fishermen were so helpless that she could hardly stop herself laughing; because when the man in the water leaned over the gunwale, all the men in the boat leaned over that side to help him, and the boat tipped over so far that they nearly fell in too. They suddenly realized what was happening and let go, and then the boat tipped the other way and they all fell on their backs.

And the crocodiles slid off the sandbank and began to swim toward them.

"Oh, pull him in, you stupid creatures!" Lila cried. "Over the end, not over the side!"

One of the fishermen heard her, and hauled the man over the stern to lie in the bottom, flopping and gasping like a fish. Meanwhile, the boat had drifted in to the side, and Lila put out a hand to stop it bumping.

As soon as they saw her, the fishermen nudged one another.

"Look," said one.

"Go *on*," muttered one of them. "*You* ask her."

"No! It was your idea! *You* do it."

"It wasn't me, it was Chang!"

"Well, he can't say anything, he's still full of water. . . ."

Finally one of them snorted with impatience and stood up, making the boat rock alarmingly. He was the stoutest man in the boat, and by far the most impressive, for he wore an ostrich plume nodding in his turban, an enormous black moustache, and a tartan sarong.

"Miss!" he said. "Would I be correct in supposing that you were hoping to cross the river?"

"Well, as a matter of fact, I was," said Lila.

He tapped his fingertips together with pleasure.

"And would I also be correct in supposing that you had a little money?"

"A little, yes," said Lila. "Could you take me across? I'll pay you."

"Look no further!" he said proudly. "Rambashi's River Taxi is at your service! I am Rambashi. Welcome aboard!"

Lila wasn't sure why a river taxi should have the name *The Bloody Murderer* painted on the bow, nor why Rambashi should be wearing no less than three daggers in his belt: one straight, one curved, and one wavy. However, there was no other way to cross the river, and so she stepped aboard, trying to avoid the man who'd been saved from drowning, who was still lying dripping in the bottom of the boat. The others took no notice of him at all, but rested their feet on him as if he were a roll of carpet.

"Cast off, my brave lads!" cried Rambashi.

Lila sat in the prow, and held the sides apprehensively as *The Bloody Murderer* swayed out into the current. Behind her she could hear the clash of oars as the blades banged together, the cries of pain as one man's handle struck another man's back, and the groaning and cursing

as the half-drowned man tried to regain his seat, but she didn't take much notice, because there was plenty to look at on the water. There were dragonflies and humming-birds, and a family of ducks out for an afternoon cruise, and crocodiles practicing looking like logs, and all sorts of things. Presently she noticed that the rowers had stopped talking, and the boat wasn't rocking unsteadily as it had been when they were rowing. In fact, it was drifting.

And the oarsmen weren't entirely silent, either. She could hear whispers:

"*You* tell her!"

"No, I don't want to. It's your turn."

"You've *got* to! You said you would!"

"Let Chang do it. It's about time he did something."

"He's not fierce enough. *You* do it!"

Lila turned round.

"Oh, for goodness' sake," she said, "what are you —"

But she didn't finish the sentence, because of the sight that met her eyes. All the rowers had put down their oars, which were sticking out in all directions, and each rower had tied a handkerchief over his nose and mouth, and they were all holding daggers. Rambashi was holding two.

They all jumped slightly when she turned round. Then they looked at Rambashi.

"Yes!" he said. "Fooled you! Ha ha! This isn't a river taxi at all. We are pirates! The fiercest pirates on the whole river. We'd cut your throat as soon as look at you."

"And drink your blood," one whispered.

"Oh yes, and drink your blood. All of it. Hand over your money, come on!"

He waved his dagger so vigorously that the boat rocked and he nearly fell out. Lila almost laughed.

"Pay up!" said Rambashi. "You're captured. Your money or your life! I warn you, we're desperate men!"

The Restaurant

Rambashi and his pirates managed to get *The Bloody Murderer* to the other bank of the river, but Lila had to fish another oar out of the water when one of them dropped it, and promise to sit still and not joggle the boat.

When they hit the bank, they all fell off their seats.

"All right," said Rambashi, picking himself up, "tie the boat to a good bit of tree or something and take the prisoner ashore."

"Are we going to eat her?" said one of the pirates. "Cause I'm hungry."

"Yes, we've had nothing to eat for days," grumbled another. "You promised we'd have a hot meal every evening."

"That's enough of that!" said Rambashi. "You're a pack of scurvy dogs. Take the prisoner up to the cave and stop complaining."

Lila wasn't sure if she could run away *just* yet; some of those pirates did look fierce enough to run after her. Though now that she looked more closely, she saw that their daggers were made of wood wrapped in silver paper, so they wouldn't be able to do her much damage.

"I hope you don't mind this little transaction," Rambashi said, as they walked along a jungle trail. "It's purely business."

"Have you kidnapped me, then?" said Lila.

"I'm afraid so. You're going to have to hand over all your money in a minute, and then we'll tie you up and hold you for ransom."

"Have you done it before?"

"Oh yes," he said. "Lots of times."

"What happens when you don't get any money?"

"Well, we . . ."

"We eat you," said the hungry pirate.

"Ssh," said Rambashi, waving his hand vaguely.

"You're not cannibals," said Lila.

"We're blooming hungry," said the pirate.

"Have you always been pirates?"

"No," said Rambashi. "I used to keep hens, but they

all died of melancholy. So I sold the business and bought the boat — Oh no! Ssh! Stop! Don't move!"

The last pirates in the line, still grumbling, bumped into those in front, who stood behind Rambashi, transfixed with fear.

For there on the path ahead of them was a tiger. It swung its tail lazily from side to side, and raised its golden eyes at them, and then opened its mouth and roared so loudly that Lila thought the very earth was shaking. One of the smallest pirates put his hand in hers.

So there they stood, and the tiger was just gathering his strength to spring, when Lila suddenly remembered her self-igniting Crackle Dragons. She took her hand back from the small pirate, reached into her bag, and took out the three she'd brought with her.

"Look out," she said to Rambashi, and pulling the string of the first one, she threw the firework in front of the tiger.

The mighty beast had never been so surprised in his life. First one, then another, then yet another Crackle Dragon snapped and flashed and sparked and leaped at him, and that was too much: With a whimper, the tiger turned and fled.

The pirates cheered.

"Magnificent!" cried Rambashi. "Congratulations! I was about to stab him to death, of course, but never mind."

(Lila wondered how he would have done that with his silver-paper-covered knife, but she didn't say anything.)

"And of course," Rambashi went on, "this changes everything. We can't keep you hostage if you've just saved our lives. You'll have to be our guest instead. Stay with us overnight, why don't you?"

"We've got no food," said someone. "What's she going to eat?"

"We'll send Chang out to catch some fish," said Rambashi cheerfully, shaking his head at the protests that rose. "No, no, fish is *good* for you. Go on, Chang! Don't just stand there!"

"I can't," said Chang. "Look."

They looked back at the river bank. *The Bloody Murderer* was drifting away, with the rope drifting in the water.

"Who tied it up?" said Rambashi.

One of the pirates looked down and tried to rub a hole in the ground with his big toe.

"Hmm," said Rambashi. "Fine pirates *you* are. I hope you're ashamed. But never mind! I've got a better idea. Miss!" he said to Lila, rubbing his hands. There was a bright gleam in his eye. "Can I interest you in a little investment?"

"Well," Lila said, "I really ought to be getting on."

"No, really, this is a *much* better idea than piracy," Rambashi said. "It came to me in a flash, just as I saw the boat floating away. (I can't be cross with these fellows, they're like children, really.) Yes, all my best

ideas come in a flash. And this one's truly brillant! Can't fail!"

"Is there any food in it?" said a pirate sourly.

"My dear boy! It's *built* on food! Just wait till you hear — I say! Miss! Just a little money — the safest investment you'll ever make —"

But Lila had walked away. As she went along the path she could hear his voice behind her. "No, listen, boys — I know where we went wrong last time. I saw it in a flash. But this is an idea that'll suit your talents down to the ground. Look, let me draw you a picture. . . ."

Lila would have liked to know what Rambashi's next plan was, but she was eager to hurry on. Mount Merapi was smoking and rumbling in the distance. She felt her heart lift when she saw it again, so powerful and dominating, and she thought, *I belong to that mountain, and it belongs to me!*

And on she went, with no other thoughts in her mind but that, and excitement putting a spring in her step.

Meanwhile, Chulak was getting ready to smuggle Hamlet out of his new home. The master had gone to

bed early, groaning, but the slaves were still awake, and Chulak had to distract them.

"Now listen," he said to them in the kitchen. "You know you've got to do all you can to please the great white elephant, or else the king'll be cross?"

They all nodded.

"Well, the elephant's a bit restless. He never sleeps well the first night in a new place, so we'll have to play a game of Elephant's Footsteps to cheer him up. You have to go and cover your eyes in the garden, and when you think you can hear him coming, turn around. He likes playing that. Go on, go and wait in the garden and I'll tell him when you're ready."

The slaves all streamed out of the back door, and as soon as they were hiding in the garden with their eyes shut, Chulak unlocked the front door and led Hamlet out to the gate.

"It's a good thing they put down that carpet I ordered," he whispered. "You don't make such a racket on the gravel."

"Can we go past the zoo?" Hamlet whispered.

"No, of course not! Never mind Frangipani. It's Lila

we've got to think about. And stop breathing so heavily. . . ."

They tiptoed out of the gate, and found Lalchand waiting there with a tarpaulin, just as Chulak had asked.

"What's it for?" Lalchand whispered.

"For this," said Chulak, and made Hamlet kneel down to have it laid over his back. "So he doesn't show up so much in the dark," Chulak told Lalchand.

"Huh," grumbled Hamlet. "It's hot and scratchy and it smells like a circus tent. Couldn't you find a nice blanket?"

"I don't think you realize your own size," Chulak said.

"Do be careful!" said Lalchand. "I ought to come with you — it's not a safe journey at all — oh, I should have told Lila everything from the start! I should have trusted her! What a foolish old man I am!"

"Yes," said Chulak. "Still, never mind. We'll find her. Come on, Hamlet!"

And they set off. Lalchand stood watching them for a minute, until they'd disappeared in the dark streets.

But someone was watching Lalchand.

One of the slaves who'd come to play Elephant's

Footsteps was hiding under a bush nearby; and as soon as he realized what he'd seen, he began to tremble. Helping the white elephant to escape was a terrible crime. There'd be a terrible punishment — and there might be a great reward for the person who pointed out the criminal.

So when Lalchand began to trudge homeward, the slave silently followed him to find out who he was and where he lived.

Chulak and Hamlet walked all night, and when morning came they slept in a little valley under some thick trees. In the afternoon they woke up, and while Hamlet browsed on the leaves Chulak went to the nearest village to ask the way to the Emerald Lake. He came back with an armful of bananas and some news.

"Guess what, Hamlet? We're in luck! This is the night of the full moon. The Water Goddess comes out of the lake and grants people's wishes. Couldn't be better, my boy! Finish your leaves and let's be moving."

They weren't the only people going to the Emerald Lake. The jungle paths were busy with families carrying picnic baskets, and even a troop of monkeys was heading in the same direction. Just before the sun set, Chulak and

Hamlet saw a young man busily pinning up notices on the trees beside the path.

Chulak was about to read one when the young man caught sight of him.

"Hey! I know you!" he said. "And him . . ."

"We know lots of people," said Chulak. "Is this the right way for the Emerald Lake?"

"Just along there. Here, can I . . ." The young man looked bashful.

Chulak knew what he wanted.

"Kneel down, Hamlet," he said. "Customer."

Hamlet couldn't say anything with the young man there, but he gave Chulak a severe look as he knelt down. The young man daubed something on Hamlet's side with a stick and some mud, and gave Chulak a coin.

"Thanks!" he said. "Wait till I tell the boss!"

And he ran off. Chulak read what he'd written:

EAT AT RAMBASHI'S JUNGLE GRILL

"Rambashi?" Chulak said. "I've got an uncle Rambashi. He used to be a chicken farmer."

The notices on the trees were advertising the Jungle

Grill as well. It was opening that very night, and there were meals at half price if you brought in a voucher from one of the notices.

"It'll be nice to see Uncle Rambashi again," Chulak said. "Come on, it'll be dark in a minute."

They hurried on. Soon they came out on the shores of the Emerald Lake. Under the trees at the edge of the water there stood some houses on stilts, with cooking fires and colored lanterns, and as the tropical darkness covered the sky in less than five minutes, Chulak and Hamlet entered the village.

Naturally, a white elephant with an advertisement written on him caused a sensation, and soon Chulak and Hamlet were being followed by a crowd of excited children and some older people with nothing else to do. Even the troupe of dancers getting into their costumes for the ceremony couldn't resist, and the dancing mistress had to run after them with her mouth full of safety pins to pull them back and scold them.

"Which way to Rambashi's Jungle Grill?" Chulak asked, and someone pointed along the shore to where a wooden building stood on stilts over the water. There was also a terrace with colored flags, and tables with

checkered tablecloths, and lamps made out of wine bot-
tles, and a cloud of smoke was coming from the kitchen,
with the sounds of sizzling and bubbling and the smell of
grilling meat and fish and spices.

"Just in time, Hamlet! What d'you think of that?
And that's Uncle Rambashi!" said Chulak.

Rambashi, wearing a white apron over his tartan
sarong, was ushering some customers on to the terrace
when he saw Chulak.

"Chulak! My boy! How delightful to see you! And
your — your friend — your pet — this excellent mobile
advertising billboard! Come in, dear boy! Voucher? Oh,
don't bother with that. Free food for everyone, in honor of
the Ceremony of the Full Moon! (Of course I'll lose money
on it, but we'll soon make it up. Wonderful publicity.) Yes,
that's right, ladies and gentlemen! Free meals tonight!"

"What about us?" said a waiter. "When do we get our
supper?"

"Customers first," said Rambashi. "You and the boys
can have as much as you like later on."

"I thought you were in the chicken business?" said
Chulak, helping himself to a big plate of prawns and rice
in satay sauce.

"Yes, but I had to give that up. I felt sorry for the hens, Chulak. So we took to the transport business for a while — river taxi, you know, with some freelance work on the side — but then came the opportunity to invest in the restaurant trade — where my talents truly lie, Chulak! — Yes, madam, our grilled lake trout is exquisite tonight — may I suggest some saffron rice to accompany it? And a flask of jasmine wine? Yes, all free. No charge! Compliments of the house . . ."

The Jungle Grill was certainly doing good business — or would be if Rambashi was charging for it.

"I hope he knows what he's doing, Hamlet," Chulak said, as the elephant browsed quietly on the banyan tree that overspread the terrace. "He reckons it'll be such good publicity that they'll come back when he starts charging. I'm not so sure. Still, the food's good. Smoky, but tasty."

Rambashi's cook was having trouble with the grill, over which he kept having to throw water when it got too hot. Clouds of smoke and steam kept billowing out, and the waiters rushed to and fro with full plates and emptied plates and flasks of wine and menus and coconuts full of ice cream.

Meanwhile, the village elders were preparing the lakeshore for the Full Moon Ceremony. Chulak and Hamlet, full of supper, wandered along to have a look. The sand was swept and smoothed, lanterns were hung in the trees, and blossoms of all colors were scattered on the water. The path from the temple to the lake was crowded several deep on either side, and Chulak had to climb on Hamlet's back in order to see.

Then the ceremony began. A great drum sounded three times, and an orchestra began to play: gongs and xylophones and drums and cymbals and flutes. A line of dancers came out of the temple and swayed down the path toward the lake, their fingernails snapping and flicking like fireflies and their golden skirts shimmering in the lantern light.

The headman of the village struck a light and lit a scented candle in a paper boat, which he floated out on to the lake. The incense made the air sweet and rich. Very soon other paper boats were floating out to join it, and then a little child pointed at the tree tops on the far side of the dark lake and said, "Moon!"

The full moon was rising. And as it rose the music

rose too, the gongs and the xylophones and the cymbals all summoning the goddess from the lake.

And then she was there, though no one had seen her arrive; it was as if she'd come when they were looking away, and when they looked back they saw her — though no one had really looked away. She was floating to the shore on a raft of water lilies, a beautiful lady in a robe the color of the moon, with silver rings and amulets, and a necklace of jasmine flowers.

One after another the villagers bowed to her and asked her help: this woman for a sick child, that man for a good harvest, these lovers for a blessing on their marriage. The goddess rebuked some for asking too much, though she never refused anyone in need. When they had all finished, and the goddess was about to depart, Chulak gathered his wits and shook his head, because he was a little dazzled by her beauty, and he thrust his way to the water's edge and knelt down.

"Goddess!" he said. "Please hear me too!"

But before the goddess could answer, hands took him roughly and hauled him away.

"What are you doing, stranger?"

"Away with him! Defiling the lake!"

"Who is he? Who gave him permission?"

"Stone him! Turn him out!"

Chulak struggled. He could see Hamlet raising his trunk and shifting his feet, and he knew the elephant was getting angry.

"No!" he cried. "Listen! I've got a special request! Let me just ask the goddess!"

The high priest looked down, frowning. His face was shadowed and stern.

"How dare you come to this sacred place?" he said. "The Goddess of the Lake is not to be disturbed by your frivolous requests. Take him away! No! She shall not hear you! Be thankful we let you go with your life. Take him to the village boundary, and if he comes back, kill him!"

The Mountain

Over the noise of the shouts and the struggle there came a sound like a mighty trumpet, and everyone fell still in fear. Chulak was frightened as well, though he knew what it was; for when Hamlet trumpeted, it meant he had nearly lost his temper.

But before anyone could move, the goddess herself spoke. Her voice was soft and low, like the murmur of waves on a beach at night.

"What is the cause of all this commotion? Stop fighting at once. It is good of you to protect me from embarrassment, High Priest, but I should like to hear from this young man, and to see his friend the elephant. Come down to the water, both of you."

Chulak looked at Hamlet, and saw that the great beast was embarrassed as well. Hamlet stepped through the crowd, being very careful not to tread on any toes,

and knelt down next to Chulak on the sand. The slogans daubed on him were very clear in the moonlight. The goddess read them, and asked Hamlet to turn around and show his other side.

"Eat at Rambashi's Jungle Grill. . . . Chang loves Lotus Blossom. . . ."

"I thought I'd washed that one off," Chulak said.

"I think it's charming," said the goddess. "But you mustn't do it any more. Your friend is too wise and noble to be written on, and if he could speak I'm sure you'd realize that yourself."

And she looked at Chulak in such a way that he knew exactly what she meant, and felt ashamed.

"However," she went on, "I can see that your request is not a frivolous one. Tell me what you seek."

"We've got a friend," Chulak said eagerly, "and she wants to be a firework-maker, you see. And she's done all the apprenticeship, but she wants to get some royal sulphur from Razvani the Fire-Fiend so as to qualify properly. So she's gone off by herself to Mount Merapi, only she didn't know about getting a flask of magic water for protection, and we don't want her to get hurt, so we've come to ask, please, as a great favor, if you could give us

some, and then we'll chase after her and see if we can catch up with her."

The goddess nodded. "Your friend has good friends," she said. "But Mount Merapi is far away, and the journey is dangerous. You had better set off at once. And take great care!"

And as if she had known what they wanted all the time, she held out a little gourd fastened with a silver clasp. Chulak took it and bowed again, and the orchestra began to play and the dancers to dance, and when people looked at the lake again the goddess was gone, though no one had seen her vanish.

Before they left, Chulak washed Hamlet clean in the lake. Some of the village children helped, but they didn't help for long, because soon there was something else for them to see: a great cloud of smoke and flames coming from the Jungle Grill.

"Oh dear, oh dear," said Chulak. "There goes Uncle Rambashi's latest plan, Hamlet. I could tell that cook was having trouble. I hope he's all right."

"They're all safe," said Hamlet. "And the children are enjoying the fire."

Squeals of delight and excitement were coming from

the crowd as the roof fell in with a shower of sparks. Buckets of water were being passed from the lake, and Chulak could hear Rambashi saying, "What a spectacle! What a splendid sight! D'you know, my boys, that gives me my best idea yet. All we have to do —"

"We haven't even had our meal!" cried one of the waiters.

"Time to go, Hamlet," said Chulak, and they set off along the lakeshore toward the mountains in the distance.

By this time, Lila had come to the end of the jungle. Climbing all the time, she moved on and on, as the trees thinned out and the path became a mere track and then vanished altogether. All the jungle sounds, the clicking and buzzing of the insects, the cries of the birds and monkeys, the drip of water off the leaves, the croaking of the little frogs, were behind her now. There was nothing to be heard except the sound of her feet on the path and the occasional rumble from the mountain, which was so deep that she felt it through her feet as much as she heard it through her ears.

When night fell she lay down on the stony ground

beside a rock and wrapped herself in her one blanket. The full moon shone right in her face and kept her awake, and she couldn't get comfortable because of the stones on the ground, and finally she sat up in annoyance.

But there was no one to share her annoyance with. She'd never felt so lonely.

"I wonder . . ." she began to say, but shook her head. She hadn't come on this journey in order to wonder how things were at home. It was the way things were at home that had made her come on the journey, after all.

"Well, if I can't sleep, I might as well keep walking," she said to herself.

She folded her blanket away and retied her sarong and tightened her sandals, and set off again.

The ground became steeper and steeper. Soon she could no longer see the top of Mount Merapi, so she knew she must be climbing the side of it. There were no plants at all here, not even shrubs or grass — just bare rock and loose stones. And the ground was warm.

"I'm close," she said to herself. "It can't be far now —"

But as she said that, she set her foot on a stone and it

rolled under her weight and she fell, and a dozen other rocks rolled down with her.

All the breath was knocked out of her, and she had none left to cry out with as the rocks pummeled and battered her.

The rocks bounded on down the mountain until finally they came to rest a long way below. Lila sat up gingerly.

"Ow," she said. "That was silly. I wasn't looking where I was putting my feet. I must be more careful."

She got up, and found that one of her shoes had come off, and had tumbled down the mountain with the stones. It was nowhere to be seen. Very delicately she put her naked foot down, and found the ground hot beneath it.

Well, there was nothing she could do about that. And hadn't she come seeking fire? And hadn't she burned herself time and again as an apprentice? And what did she need delicate feet for anyway?

On she climbed, higher and higher. Before long she came to a part of the slope where all the stones were loose, and where she slid back two steps for every three she took upward. Her feet and legs were bruised and battered, and then she lost her other sandal; and she nearly cried

out in despair, because there was no sign of the grotto, just an endless slope of hot rough stones that tumbled and rolled underfoot.

And her throat was parched and her lungs were panting in the hot thin air, and she fell to her knees and clung with trembling fingers as the stones began to roll under her again. She let go her little bag of food and her blanket; they didn't matter anymore. The only thing that mattered was climbing on. She dragged herself on bleeding knees up and up, until every muscle hurt, until she

had no breath left in her lungs, until she thought she was going to die; and still she went on.

Then one stone bigger than the rest began to shift above her as the little stones beneath it tumbled down. It slid and rolled toward her and she had no strength to move, but at the last second it bounded over her and rolled on down the mountainside in a cloud of dust and pebbles.

Where it had been, there was a great hole as tall as a house. The moonlight shone into it a little way, but the hole went deeper still, right into the heart of the mountain. A gust of sulphur-laden smoke came billowing out, and Lila knew she had found her goal: It was the Grotto of the Fire-Fiend.

Razvani

She pulled herself up with shaking arms, and stepped inside. The floor was baking hot and the air was hardly breathable. She walked on, deeper into the earth, deeper than the moonlight went, and heard nothing but silence, and saw nothing but dark rock.

Harsh, barren walls rose to left and right; she felt them with her bleeding hands. Then the tunnel opened out into a great cavern. She had never seen anything so gloomy and empty of life, and her heart sank, because she had come all this way and there was nothing here.

She sank to the floor.

And, as if that were a signal, a little flame licked out of the rocky wall for an instant, and went out.

Then another, in a different place.

Then another.

Then the earth shook and groaned, and with a harsh

grating sound, the rocky wall tore itself open, and suddenly the cavern was full of light.

Lila sat up, astonished, as red fire and flame licked and crackled at the rocky roof. All of a sudden, the grotto was alive with movement, as a thousand fire-imps swarmed upward to dash themselves against the rock and smash into a thousand more, as a wide carpet of boiling lava spread from side to side, as the clang and clash of great hammers and anvils rang with the rhythm of a great fire-dance.

The cavern was full of light and noise, as thousands upon thousands of little fire-spirits toiled and blazed and swung hammers, and ran to and fro with handfuls of sparks, and swarmed against the rocky wall till it melted and slid downward like soft wax. Then the greedy creatures plunged their red hands into it and lifted up the bubbling sulphur to their tiny mouths and ate and ate until another mass of rock slid down and smothered them.

And then into the heart of the light and the fire and the noise leaped Razvani himself, the great Fire-Fiend, whose body was a mass of flame and whose face a mask of scorching light.

Thousands of fire-imps scattered as he landed, and even the blazing flames bowed down to him. And so did Lila.

In a voice like the roar of a forest fire, Razvani spoke.

"By what right have you come to my grotto?"

She swallowed hard. It was difficult to breathe, because she seemed to be taking fire into her lungs as well as air.

"I want to be a firework-maker," she managed to say.

He laughed a great laugh.

"You? Never! And what do you want from me?"

"Royal sulphur," she gasped.

At that he slapped his sides and laughed even harder, and a chorus of jeers and shrieks of merriment burst from all the fire-imps.

"The royal sulphur? Did you hear that? Oh, that's good! That's funny! Well, speak, girl: Have you the Three Gifts?"

Lila could only shrug and shake her head. She could hardly speak.

"I don't know what they are," she said.

"So what were you going to exchange for the royal sulphur?" he roared.

"I don't know!"

"You were going to give *nothing* in exchange?"

She had nothing to say. She bowed her head.

"Well, you've come this far," said the fire-fiend, "and there's no going back. Now that you're here, you must walk in the flames, like every other firework-maker. I expect you've brought some magic water from my cousin, the Goddess of the Lake? You've brought nothing for me, but I don't suppose you've forgotten to take care of yourself. Better drink it quickly!"

"I've got nothing!" Lila gasped. "I didn't know about magic water or the Three Gifts — I just wanted to be a firework-maker! And I'll be a good one, Razvani! I invented self-igniting Crackle Dragons and Leaping Monkeys! I've learned everything my father could teach me! It's all I want — to be a firework-maker like him!"

But Razvani merely laughed.

"Show her the ghosts!" he cried, and clapped his blazing hands.

Instantly a crack shivered its way down the rock wall, and out of the opening came a procession of ghosts, each attended by fire-demons. The ghosts were so pale and

transparent that Lila could hardly see them, but she heard them wailing.

"Beware! Look at me! I came without the Three Gifts!"

"Alas! Take warning from me! I hadn't worked at the craft and I wasn't ready!"

"Maiden, turn back! I was arrogant and headstrong! I didn't seek the water from the goddess, and I perished in the flames!"

Wailing and weeping, the ghosts passed across the lake of fire, and vanished into a crack in the opposite wall.

"That's what happens to those who don't come prepared!" said Razvani. "But now you must submit yourself as they did. Walk into my flames, Lila! You have come for the royal sulphur — receive it from my hands!"

And he laughed louder, and spun in a rapid dance, stamping his feet in a wide circle and causing a ring of fire to blaze up around him. Through the lashing red and yellow and orange, his face seemed to waver and flicker, but his voice rang out clearly over the roar and crackle: "You want to be a firework-maker? Walk into my flames! Your father did in his time, and so did every

artist in fire. This is what you've come for! Why are you waiting?"

She was terribly afraid. But she knew that she must do it; she would rather be a ghost than go back empty-handed and fail at the one thing she had ever wanted.

So she took one step forward, and then another, and her poor feet burned and blistered so that she cried out loud. Then she took another step, and when she knew she could bear it no longer she heard a great sound behind her, like a mighty trumpet. And through the blaze a voice was shouting, "Lila! The water! Take it, take it!"

And there was a small figure beside her, thrusting something into her hands: a gourd! A drinking gourd with a clasp that she tore off, before lifting it to her parched lips and drinking, drinking, drinking deep.

All at once a marvelous coolness spread through her body and down to the tips of her toes. The pain vanished and the dryness in her throat and lungs was soothed and moistened.

At the entrance to the cave behind her she could see Chulak, shrinking back and covering his face from the heat, and she could see Hamlet fanning him with his ears.

But she was in the heart of the fire, facing Razvani once again, and the flames were harmless now. They played like fountains of light; they rushed up her legs and arms and across her face like darting birds and she felt light and joyful as if she were a flame herself, dancing with pure energy and joy.

"So you have done it!" Razvani said to her. "Welcome to the flames, Lila."

"And . . . the royal sulphur?" she said.

"Ah, when you reach the heart of the fire, all your illusions vanish. Didn't your father tell you that?"

"Illusions? I don't understand!"

"The royal sulphur doesn't exist, Lila. There is no such thing!"

"Then . . . how can I be a firework-maker? I thought every firework-maker needed some royal sulphur to become a true artist!"

"Illusions, Lila. Fire burns away all our illusions. The world itself is all illusion. Everything that exists flickers like a flame for a moment, and then vanishes. The only thing that lasts is change itself. There is no royal sulphur. All illusion . . . everything outside the fire is illusion!"

"But the Three Gifts — I don't understand! What are the Three Gifts, Razvani?"

"Whatever they are, you must have brought them to me," he said.

And that was the last thing she heard from him, for as he said that he dwindled away, and the lake of fire darkened and became red rock, and then just rock, and all the myriad fire-imps became little feeble sparks that floated aimlessly for a second, and sank, and went out at once.

The grotto was bare again.

Lila turned away from where the fire had been. She was dazed and disappointed, calm and curious, pleased and puzzled; in fact, she didn't know what she felt or who she was for a moment. But then she saw Chulak and ran to him.

"Chulak, you saved my life! And you're hurt — you're burned — let me help you!"

He was shaking his head and tugging at her hand.

"Don't waste any time," he said. "We've got to hurry. Tell her as we go, Hamlet!"

They stumbled out of the grotto into the pale light of dawn, and Hamlet said, "I'm sorry, Lila. I heard the birds talking at the foot of the mountain, and they said 'Look! The white elephant! That's the very one who escaped from the city!' And I asked the bird what he knew, and he said 'The firework-maker helped you to escape. Someone saw and told the king, and now Lalchand has been arrested, and he's going to be executed!' Then he flew away to tell the other birds. Lila, we've got to go back as fast as we can. Don't waste time blaming anyone! Get on my back and hold tight."

So, in a torment of fear that put Razvani and the royal sulphur and the Three Gifts completely out of her mind, Lila clambered up next to Chulak on the elephant's back, and held on tight as Hamlet began to slither down the mountain in the light of dawn.

Judgment

How they did it Lila never knew. They stopped only for Hamlet to drink deeply from the river while Lila and Chulak snatched some fruit from the trees over- hanging the bank, but after hours and hours of pounding and trudging and half-running on blistered feet, they came to the outskirts of the city. The sun was setting.

Of course, Hamlet attracted a lot of attention as soon as he was seen, because everyone knew that the white elephant had escaped. Soon they were surrounded by a curious crowd, all trying to touch Hamlet for luck, and before they'd got anywhere near the palace, they could move no further.

Lila was nearly weeping with fear and impatience.

"Have they killed my father yet? Is Lalchand still alive?" she asked, but no one knew.

"Move out of the way!" Chulak shouted. "Clear a space there! Make room!"

But they could only move forward an inch at a time. Chulak could feel Hamlet getting angry, and he feared he wouldn't be able to control him. He stroked the elephant's trunk to try and keep him calm.

Then they heard shouts and the clash of swords from somewhere ahead, and the crowd parted at once. Word had reached the palace, and the king had sent his Special and Particular Bodyguard to escort Hamlet back to his royal home.

"About time too!" said Chulak to the general in charge. "Come on, we're in a hurry. Clear the streets and stand aside."

So the three of them, burned and blistered and dusty and exhausted, were escorted into the palace by the splendidly uniformed bodyguards, who tried to look as if they'd found Hamlet all by themselves. Poor Lila's heart was beating like a bird caught in a net.

"Prostrate yourselves!" said the Special and Particular General. "Grovel! Faces to the ground! Especially yours, boy."

They knelt on the stones of the courtyard in the light

of flaming torches and the Special and Particular Guard lined up to present arms as the king came in.

His Majesty stood in front of them. Lila could see his golden sandals, and then her anxiety got too much for her, and she knelt up and said in anguish, "Please, Your Majesty — my father, Lalchand — you haven't — he isn't — is he still alive?"

The king looked down sternly.

"He will die tomorrow morning," he said. "There is only one penalty for what he has done."

"Oh, please! Please spare his life! It was all my fault, not his at all! I ran away without telling him and — "

"Enough," said the king, and he was so frightening that she stopped, just like that.

Then he turned to Chulak.

"Who are you?" he said.

Chulak got up at once, but before he could begin to speak a Special and Particular Guard forced him down again.

"I'm Chulak, Your Majesty," he said. "Can I look up? It's not easy to speak with a foot on my neck."

The king nodded, and the guard stood back. Chulak knelt up beside Lila and said, "That's better. You see,

Your Majesty, I'm the elephant's Special and Particular Groom, in a manner of speaking. He's a delicate beast, and if he's handled wrong there's no end of trouble. And as soon as I found out he'd escaped I set off at once, Your Majesty. I swam across the river and I climbed mountains and fought my way through the jungle and —"

Suddenly all the breath was knocked from Chulak's body and he sprawled on the ground again. Something soft had knocked him in the middle of the back, and he knew it was Hamlet's trunk. Hamlet had never done that to him before, and he rolled over in surprise to see the elephant giving him a special and particular look, and then he realized what he must do.

He struggled up again and faced the king.

"Your Majesty, the elephant has just made a request. Him and me have got this unusual way of communicating, you see. He is asking for an audience alone with Your Majesty."

Even the Special and Particular General could hardly restrain a snigger at the idea of an animal asking to speak to the king, but he changed it into a cough when the king glared at him.

"Alone?" the king said to Chulak.

"Yes, Your Majesty."

"The white elephant is a rare and wondrous beast," the king said. "For his sake I shall grant his request. And if it turns out that you are playing a joke on me, you may be certain that tomorrow morning you will have very little to laugh about. General, take these two outside and leave me alone with the elephant."

The guards hauled Lila and Chulak out of the court-yard and into the kitchen compound where the smell of grilling meat and spices reminded them both that they hadn't had a meal for twenty-four hours.

"Don't worry," said Chulak. "Hamlet will explain everything."

"Is he going to *talk* to the king, then? I thought his talking was a great secret!"

"These are special and particular circumstances. Oh, that rice! Oh, that plum sauce! Oh, the smell of those spices!"

And even Lila's fear couldn't prevent her mouth from watering, she was so hungry.

And then they waited. Minutes went by, and more

minutes, and poor Lila was so stiff and tired she nearly fell asleep standing up, as worried as she was. But finally there was a stir of movement by the door.

"Prisoners!" barked the general. "Fall in and follow me!"

Two lines of guardsmen all stamping proudly, with Chulak and Lila between them, followed the general back to the courtyard.

When they had bowed properly the king said "Firstly, as for you, Chulak, I am suspending my judgment. I have it on good authority that you have never sought to harm the elephant, but I am not convinced that you are the best person to look after him. You are dismissed."

Chulak swallowed hard, and looked at Hamlet.

Then the king turned to Lila and said, "I have considered your case very carefully. It is highly unusual, and this is my decision. I shall spare the life of Lalchand the Firework-Maker, but only on one condition. Next week, as the whole city knows, we celebrate the Festival of the New Year, and I have invited the greatest artists in fireworks from all over the world to contribute to a display.

"Now here is my plan: I shall announce a competition

for the final night of the festival. A firework display will be put on by each of my invited artists, and Lalchand and Lila will take part as well. The prize of a golden cup will be awarded to the artist whose display receives the longest applause. That is all that the other competitors will know.

"But you and Lalchand will know something else as well. If your display wins, Lalchand will receive the prize and go free; but if you lose the competition, he loses his life too.

"That is my decision, and there will be no appeal. You have a week to save your father's life, Lila.

"Guards, see them out, and release Lalchand the Firework-Maker into the care of his daughter."

And Lila barely had time to think before she found herself at a little side door of the palace, where a servant held up a flickering torch for her to wait by. But she didn't have to wait long. From behind a door came the sound of a chain falling to the ground, and then the door opened and there was Lalchand.

Neither of them could speak, but they hugged each other so tightly that they could barely breathe. When they'd had enough, they realized how hungry they were, and hurried home.

"We'll get some fried prawns from the stall in the alley, and eat them as we work," said Lalchand.

"Have they told you what the king decided?" Lila asked.

"Yes. But I'm not worried. We'll have to work as we've never worked before, but we can do it. . . ."

And Lila forgot all about the royal sulphur and the Three Gifts. There was no time to wonder about them now. She hurried into the workshop with some dishes of

rice and prawns and fried vegetables, and they scooped them up absentmindedly as they worked.

"Father," said Lila, "I've got an idea. Supposing..."

She took a stick of charcoal from the bench and drew some quick sketches. Lalchand's eyes lit up.

"Aha! But begin slowly. Build up to it."

"And on the way back from Mount Merapi," she said, "when we stopped by the river, I saw how some vines had twisted around each other, and I thought of a way of delaying the fuses. Making them burn at different rates."

"Impossible!"

"It isn't. Look, I'll show you. . . ."

And so they set to work.

The Contest

The invited firework-makers arrived the very next day, together with all the other famous artists and performers: the Chinese Scout and Guide Opera Company, Señor Archibaldo Gomez and his Filipino Mambo Orchestra, the Norwegian National Comedy Cowbell Players, and many others. They all disembarked from the *S.S. Indescribable* with their luggage and their instruments and their costumes, and began to rehearse at once.

The first firework-maker was Dr. Puffenflasch, from Heidelberg. He had invented a multistage rocket which exploded at a height of two thousand feet into the shape of a gigantic frankfurter sausage, while a huge instrument he'd invented played "The Ride of the Valkyries." Herr Puffenflasch had gone to immense trouble to prepare something just as spectacular for the New Year

Festival, and he supervised the unloading of his enormous equipment with scrupulous care.

The second visiting firework-maker was Signor Scorcini from Naples. His family had been making fireworks for generations, and his speciality was noise. For this display he had invented a full-scale representation of a battle at sea, featuring the noisiest fireworks in the world, and with King Neptune emerging from the water to see fair play and declare peace.

The third and last firework-maker was Colonel Sam Sparkington from Chicago. His display was called "The Greatest Firework Show in the Galaxy," and it usually featured Colonel Sparkington himself, wearing a white Stetson hat and riding a horse. This time, it was rumored, he had invented an especially exciting display, involving something never before seen in the art of pyrotechnics.

And while the three visiting firework-makers were assembling their displays, Lalchand and Lila were working on theirs. Time flew past. They barely slept, they scarcely washed, they hardly ate. They mixed vats of Golden Serpents, they ordered a ton and a half of flowers of salt, they invented something so new neither could

think of a name for it until Lila said, "Foaming . . ." and snapped her fingers.

"Moss?" said Lalchand.

"That's it!"

Lila showed Lalchand her delayed-fuse method, but it didn't work until he thought of adding some spirits of saltpeter, and then it worked magnificently. It would let them set off fifty or a hundred fireworks at once, which had previously been impossible. Then Lalchand came up with a spectacular finale, but it depended on something even more impossible: burning a fuse underwater. Lila solved that by thinking of caustic naphtha, and they tried it, and it worked.

And before they knew it, the day of the festival arrived.

"I wonder where Chulak is?" Lila said vaguely, but her mind was really on the Foaming Moss.

"I hope Hamlet's being treated well," said Lalchand, but he was really thinking about the caustic naphtha.

And neither of them said anything about the king's decision, but they couldn't get it out of their minds.

After a hasty sleep and a hurried breakfast, they

loaded up the fried-prawn seller's cart (he'd lent it to them because he was taking the day off) and trundled it through the streets to the royal park, where the displays were going to take place. The batik seller followed behind with another cart, and behind him came the sandalwood carver from down the street with a third, all laden with fireworks.

But when they reached the ornamental lake, Lila and Lalchand stopped in dismay.

For there was Dr. Puffenflasch supervising the final stages of putting together about fifteen tons of equipment, all swathed in a neat tarpaulin, and swarmed over by a dozen pyrotechnicians in white overalls, with clipboards and stethoscopes.

And next to him there was Signor Scorcini clambering about on a model galleon even longer than the royal barge, all bristling with cannons and flares, while his Neapolitan crew were arguing and gesticulating in a Neapolitan dialect as they lowered a vast, nodding, bearded model of King Neptune below the water.

And next to him Colonel Sparkington was rehearsing his display. There was a gigantic red, white, and blue rocket with a saddle on the back of it, and on a scaffold-

ing platform high above the treetops there was a model of the moon, with dozens of craters all being loaded with exciting-looking things. . . .

It was too much. Lalchand and Lila looked at the vast displays being prepared by the other artists, and then at their little three cartloads, and their hearts sank.

"Never mind," said Lalchand. "Ours is a good display, my love. Think of the Foaming Moss! They've got nothing like that."

"Or the underwater fuse," said Lila. "Look, they're having to light that sea god by hand. We can do better than that, Father!"

"Of course we can. Let's get to work. . . ."

They unloaded their materials, and the batik painter and the sandalwood carver took their carts back, with the promise of free tickets to the show.

The day passed quickly. All the firework-makers were very curious about one another's displays, and kept wandering over to have a look, with the excuse of borrowing a handful of red fire powder or a length of slow fuse. They came to look at Lalchand and Lila's, and they were very polite, but it was plain that they didn't think much of it.

And all of them were desperate to look under Dr. Puffenflasch's tarpaulin, but he kept it tightly tied down.

Promptly at seven o'clock the sun went down, and ten minutes later it was dark. People were beginning to arrive already, with rugs to sit on and picnic baskets, and from the palace nearby came the sound of bells and gongs and cymbals. All the firework-makers were busy in the dark, putting the finishing touches to their displays, and they all wished one another good luck.

Then came a roll of drums, and the palace gates were thrown open. By the light of a hundred flickering torches, a great procession made its way to the grandstand by the lake. The king was being carried in a golden palanquin, and the royal dancers were swaying and stepping elegantly alongside. Behind them, decorated with gold cloths and jewels of every color, with his tusks and toenails painted scarlet, came Hamlet.

"Oh, look at the poor thing!" said Lila. "He looks utterly miserable. I'm sure he's lost weight."

"He's missing Chulak, that's what it is," said Lalchand.

Hamlet stood disconsolately beside the grandstand as the king declared the competition open.

"A prize of a gold cup and a thousand gold coins will be awarded to the winner!" the king proclaimed. "Only your applause will decide who has won. The first contestant will now begin his display."

The firework-makers had drawn lots to see which order they'd perform in. Dr. Puffenflasch was first. Of course the audience had no idea what to expect, and when his mighty rockets whizzed up into the night sky, and his gigantic *Bombardenorgelmitsparkenpumpe* began to play "The Ride of the Valkyries," hurling out great lumps of Teutonic lava, they all burst into oohs and aahs of excitement. Then came the highlight of his display. Out of the darkness arose a tribute to the king's favorite dish: a gigantic pink prawn, fizzing and sputtering, which began to revolve faster and faster until it all went out in a shower of salmon-colored sparks and a sonorous chord from the *Bombardenorgelmitsparkenpumpe*.

The applause was colossal.

"That was good," said Lila apprehensively. "That big prawn. Really ... *big*. And pink."

"A bit too obvious," said Lalchand. "Don't worry. Nice pink, though. Must ask him for the recipe."

The next to go was Signor Scorcini with his

Neapolitan pyrotechnicians. Red, green, and white rockets whizzed up in the air to explode with enormous bangs that echoed all around the city, and then the galleon came ablaze with sparklers and Catherine wheels, and a chorus of galley slaves made of Roman candles moved their oars stiffly to and fro. Suddenly a giant octopus rose up out of the water, waving ghastly green tentacles, and attacked the ship. The sailors fired all kinds of Jumping Jacks and Whizzers and Incandescent Fountains at it, and then they tipped cascades of Greek Fire over it from barrels lashed to the masts. The noise was indescribable. Just when it looked as if the ship was about to tip over, up came King Neptune, waving his trident, accompanied by three mermaids. The band struck up, and the mermaids sang a jolly Euro-song called "Boom Bang-a-Bang," the octopus waved its tentacles in time, and more rockets went off in rhythm with the music.

The audience loved it. They roared with delight.

"Oh dear," said Lalchand. "That was very exciting. Oh dear, oh dear."

"But didn't you see how they had to light the sea god?" Lila said. "They had to wait till he was right out of

the water and a little man in a boat reached up with a match. Just wait till they see our underwater fuse!"

When the applause had died down, Colonel Sparkington's display began. First a lot of circular saucer-shaped fireworks whizzed down from the darkness and landed on the grass. That got a round of applause on its own, because fireworks usually went up, not down. Then the famous moon swung into view, way up above the treetops, and Colonel Sparkington galloped in on a white horse made of tiny Catherine wheels, waving his Stetson hat to the audience, who were in such a good mood that they cheered and cheered.

Lila could see an official beside the king carefully counting the seconds that each burst of applause lasted. She swallowed hard.

Then came the climax of Colonel Sparkington's display. After stamping out the flying saucers with his Catherine-wheel horse, the gallant colonel jumped aboard the red, white and blue rocket. A Cherokee chieftain galloped in on a palomino pony and fired a blazing arrow at the tail of the rocket, which ignited at once and whooshed up along a wire to the moon, with Colonel Sparkington waving his hat all the way.

As soon as it landed, a dozen craters flipped open and out came some little round-faced moon people with big eyes and pointed ears. The audience went wild. The moon people waved the flags of all nations and bowed to the king, Colonel Sparkington distributed rockets to them all, and they whizzed off in all directions, singing a song called "Sparkington Forever." You could hear the clapping, the cheering and whistling and stamping, for miles around.

Lila and Lalchand looked at each other. There was nothing to say. But then they hugged each other very tightly, and ran to their places, and as soon as the audience was settled again, they began their display.

The first thing that happened was that little lotus flowers made of white fire suddenly popped open on the water, with no hint of where the fire had come from. The audience fell silent, and when the flowers began to float across the dark lake like little paper boats, they were completely hushed.

Then a beautiful green light began to glow beneath the water, and rose slowly upward to become a fountain of green fire. But it didn't look like fire — it looked like water, and it splashed and danced like a bubbling spring.

And while the fountain played over the lake, something quite different was happening under the trees. A carpet of living moss seemed to have spread itself across the grass, a million million little points of light all so close together that they looked as soft as velvet. A sort of "aaah" sound came from the audience.

Then came the most difficult part. Lila had designed a sequence of fireworks based on what she had seen in the Grotto of the Fire-Fiend, but it all depended on the delayed-action fuses working as they should — and of course they hadn't had time to test them properly. If some of the fireworks went off a second too early or a second too late, the whole show would make no sense.

But there was no time to worry about that now. Quickly and expertly she and Lalchand touched fire to the end of the master fuses, and held their breath.

First came a series of slow dull explosions like the beat of a muffled drum. Everything was dark. Then a red light shivered downward, leaving a trail of red sparks hanging in the air, like a crack opening in the night. The solemn drumbeats got louder and louder, and everyone sat very still, holding their breath, because of the irresistible feeling that *something* was going to happen.

Then it did. Out of the red crack in the night a great cascade of brilliant red, orange, and yellow lava seemed to pour down and spread out like the carpet of fire in the grotto. Lila couldn't resist glancing up very swiftly at Dr. Puffenflasch, Signor Scorcini, and Colonel Sparkington, and saw them all watching wide-eyed like little children.

When the lava carpet had flowed down almost to the edge of the lake, the speed of the drumbeat got faster, and sharp bangs and cracks beat the air between them. And suddenly, dancing as he had in the grotto, Razvani himself seemed to be there, whirling and stamping and laughing for joy in the play of the eternal fire.

Both Lila and Lalchand forgot everything else, and seized each other's hands and danced as well. Never had they produced such a display! No matter what happened, it was worth it, everything was worth it, for a moment of joy like this! They laughed and danced for happiness.

But their fire was not Razvani's, of course, and it couldn't last forever. The great red firework-demon burned himself out, and the last of the red lava poured slowly into the lake, and then the little white lotus boats, now scattered over the water like the stars in the sky,

flared up and burned more brightly than ever for a moment before all going out at once.

Then there was silence. It was a silence that got longer and longer until Lila could hardly bear it, and she gripped Lalchand's hand so tightly it nearly cracked.

And when she thought it was all over, Lalchand was doomed, everything was ruined, there came a mighty yell from Colonel Sparkington.

"Yeee-haa!" he cried, waving his hat. And —

"Bravissimo!" shouted Signor Scorcini, clapping his hands above his head. And —

"Hoch! Hoch! Hoch!" roared Dr. Puffenflasch, seizing the cymbals from his *Bombardenorgelmitsparkenpumpe* in order to clap more loudly.

The audience, not to be out-applauded by the visiting firework-makers, joined in with such a roar and a stamping and a clapping and a thumping of one another on the back and a whistling and a shouting that four hundred and thirty-eight doves roosting in a tree ten miles away woke up and said, "Did you hear that?"

Of course the court official timing the applause had to give up. It was obvious to everyone who had won, and

Lalchand and Lila went up to the royal platform where the king was waiting to present the prize.

"I keep my word," the king said quietly. "Lalchand, you are free. Take this prize, the pair of you, and enjoy the festival!"

Hardly knowing what was happening, Lila and Lalchand wandered back to the darkness of the firing area under the trees. And he might have been going to say something, and she might have spoken too, but suddenly the air was filled with the sound of a mighty trumpet.

"It's Hamlet!" said Lila. "Look! He's excited about something!"

A moment later they saw what the elephant had seen, and Lila clapped her hands for joy. A little figure came strolling on to the grass in front of the royal platform and bowed elegantly to the king. It was Chulak.

"Your Majesty!" he said, and everyone stopped to hear what he was going to say. "In honor of your great wisdom and generosity to all your subjects, and in celebration of your many glorious years on the throne and in the hope of many even more glorious ones ahead, and as a

tribute to the splendor of your courage and your dignity, and in recognition . . ."

"He's on the verge of being cheeky," Lalchand said, as Chulak went on. "I can see the king tapping his foot. That's a bad sign."

". . . So, Your Majesty," Chulak finished, "I have the honor to present to you a group of the finest musicians ever heard, who will sing a selection of vocal gems, for your delight. Your Majesty, my lords, ladies and gentlemen — Rambashi's Melody Boys!"

"I don't believe it!" said Lila.

But she had to, because there were Rambashi's ex-pirates in person, wearing smart scarlet jackets and tartan sarongs. Rambashi himself, beaming all over his broad face, gave a deep bow and prepared to conduct them — but before he could begin, there was an interruption.

One of the dancing girls who had accompanied the royal procession from the Palace suddenly squealed and cried, "Chang!"

And one of the Melody Boys held out his arms and cried, "Lotus Blossom!"

"What did he say?" said Lalchand. "Locust Bottom?"

The young couple ran to each other with their arms outstretched, but stopped, embarrassed, as they realized that everyone was watching.

"Well, go on," said the king. "You might as well."

So they kissed shyly, and everyone cheered.

"And now I'd like an explanation, please," said the king.

"I was a carpenter, Your Majesty," said Chang, "and I thought I ought to seek my fortune before I asked Lotus Blossom to marry me. So I went off and sought it, and that's what I'm doing here, Your Majesty."

"Well, you'd better start singing then," said the king.

So Chang ran back to the Melody Boys, and Rambashi counted them in, and they began to sing a close-harmony song called "Down by the Old Irrawaddy."

"They're very good, aren't they?" said Lalchand.

"I'm amazed!" said Lila. "After all the trouble they've had finding the right thing to do! Who would have thought it?"

The song came to an end and the king led the applause. While Rambashi was announcing the next one, Lila went to talk to Chulak, and found him stroking

Hamlet's trunk. The elephant looked happy, but of course he couldn't say so with everyone around.

"Have you heard?" said Chulak. "Hamlet's going to get married! Oh, well done, by the way. We heard the racket they made when you won. I always knew you would. And I've got my job back!"

Hamlet cuffed him gently around the head.

"So Frangipani said yes?" said Lila. "Congratulations, Hamlet! I'm so pleased. What made her change her mind?"

"Me!" said Chulak. "I went and told her about his gallant deeds up on Mount Merapi, and she was conquered. Actually she said she'd loved him all the time, but she hadn't liked to say so. Old Uncle Rambashi's doing well, isn't he?"

The audience was clapping and cheering as Rambashi announced the next song. When the Melody Boys were singing and swaying to "Save the Last Mango for Me," Lila wandered back to Lalchand, who was deep in talk with the three other firework-makers. They all stood up politely and asked her to join them.

"I was just congratulating yer pa on that mighty fine

display," said Colonel Sparkington. "And half the credit goes to you, miss. That trick with the little bitty boats that all went out at once — that's a lulu. How d'you work that stunt?"

So Lila told them about the delayed action fuses, because there are no secrets among true artists. And Dr. Puffenflasch told them the art of pink fire, and Signor Scorcini told them how he made the octopus's legs wave, and they all talked for hours and liked one another enormously.

And very late, when they were extremely tired and when even Rambashi's Melody Boys had run out of songs to sing, Lila and Lalchand found themselves alone in the great garden, on the grass under the warm stars. Lalchand cleared his throat and looked embarrassed.

"Lila, my dear," he said, "I've got an apology to make."

"Whatever for?"

"Well, you see, I should have trusted you. I brought you up as a firework-maker's daughter; I should have expected you to want to be a firework-maker yourself. After all, you have the Three Gifts."

"Oh yes! The Three Gifts! Razvani asked if I had them, and I didn't know — but then he said I must have

brought them after all. And what with rushing back to the city and preparing the display, and worrying about whether we'd manage to save your life, I forgot all about them. And I still don't know what they are."

"Well, my dear, did you see the ghosts?" said Lalchand.

"Yes, I did. They didn't bring the gifts, and they failed. . . . But what *are* the Three Gifts?"

"They are what all firework-makers must have. They are all equally important, and two of them are no good

without the third. The first one is talent, and you have that, my dear. The second has many names: courage, determination, willpower. . . . It's what made you carry on climbing the mountain when everything seemed hopeless."

Lila was silent for a moment, and then she said, "What is the third?"

"It's simply luck," he said. "It's what gave you good friends like Chulak and Hamlet, and brought them to you in time. Those are the Three Gifts, and you took them and offered them to Razvani as a firework-maker should. And he gave you the royal sulphur in exchange."

"But he didn't!"

"Yes, he did."

"He said it was illusion!"

"In the eyes of Razvani, no doubt it is. But human beings call it wisdom. You can only gain that by suffering and risk — by taking the journey to Mount Merapi. It's what the journey is for. Each of our friends, the other firework-makers, has made his own journey in a similar way, and so has Rambashi. So you see, you didn't come home empty-handed, Lila. You did bring back the royal sulphur."

Lila thought of Hamlet and Frangipani, now happily engaged. She thought of Chulak, restored to his job, and Chang and Lotus Blossom, restored to each other. She thought of Rambashi and the Melody Boys, happily snoring in the Hotel Intercontinental, dreaming of the triumphant show-business career that lay ahead of them. She thought of the other firework-makers and how they'd welcomed her as one of them.

And then she realized what she had learned. She suddenly saw that Dr. Puffenflasch loved his pink fire, and Signor Scorcini loved his octopus, and Colonel Sparkington loved his funny moon people. To make good fireworks you had to love them, every little sparkler or Crackle Dragon. That was it! You had to put love into your fireworks as well as all the skill you had.

(And Dr. Puffenflasch's pink fire really was very pretty. If they combined some of it with a little glimmer juice, and some of that doubling-back powder they'd never found a use for, they might be able to —)

She laughed, and turned to Lalchand.

"*Now* I see!" she said.

And so it was that Lila became a firework-maker.

About the Author and the Illustrator

❊ ❊ ❊

Philip Pullman, the author of *Clockwork, or All Wound Up,* has received the highest awards given for children's literature in England — the Carnegie Medal and the Guardian Fiction Award — for *The Golden Compass*, the first book of the His Dark Materials trilogy.

Mr. Pullman graduated from Oxford University and now makes his home in Oxford, England, with his wife and two children. He writes in a shed in the garden behind his home.

S. Saelig Gallagher has received many awards and honors for her illustrations, including the Gold Medal from the Society of Illustrators. Her books include *Moonhorse* by Mary Pope Osborne and *The Selfish Giant* by Oscar Wilde.

Don't miss these other great books from Scholastic Signature.